MANCHESTER

This English edition published in 2017 under license from big & SMALL
by Eerdmans Books for Young Readers,
an imprint of Wm. B. Eerdmans Publishing Co.
2140 Oak Industrial Dr. NE, Grand Rapids, Michigan 49505
www.eerdmans.com/youngreaders

Original Korean text by Gyeong-hwa Kim • Illustrations by Anna Balbusso & Elena Balbusso • English edition edited by Joy Cowley
Original Korean edition © Yeowon Media Co., Ltd. • English edition © big & SMALL 2014

17 18 19 20 21 22 23   9 8 7 6 5 4 3 2 1

Manufactured at Tien Wah Press in Malaysia

Names: Kim, Gyeong- hwa, author. | Balbusso, Anna, 1967- illustrator. |
 Balbusso, Elena, 1967- illustrator.
Title: Leather shoe Charlie / by Gyeong-hwa Kim ; illustrated by Anna and
 Elena Balbusso.
Description: Grand Rapids, MI : Eerdmans Books for Young Readers, 2016. |
 Summary: "Charlie's dream of becoming a cobbler is threatened when his
 family moves to Manchester during the Industrial Revolution"— Provided by
 publisher.
Identifiers: LCCN 2015046913 | ISBN 9780802854735 (paperback)
Subjects: | CYAC: Shoes—Fiction. | Industrial revolution—Fiction. | Family
 life—England—Fiction. | Manchester (England)—Fiction. | Great
 Britain—History—19th century—Fiction. | BISAC: JUVENILE FICTION /
 Historical / Europe. | JUVENILE FICTION / People & Places / Europe. |
 JUVENILE FICTION / Business, Careers, Occupations.
Classification: LCC PZ7.1.K583 Le 2016 | DDC [E]—dc23
LC record available at https://lccn.loc.gov/2015046913

Display type set in Brubeck AH
Text type set in Garamond

Leather Shoe Charlie

Written by **Gyeong-hwa Kim**
Illustrated by **Anna & Elena Balbusso**
Edited by **Joy Cowley**

Eerdmans Books for Young Readers

Grand Rapids, Michigan

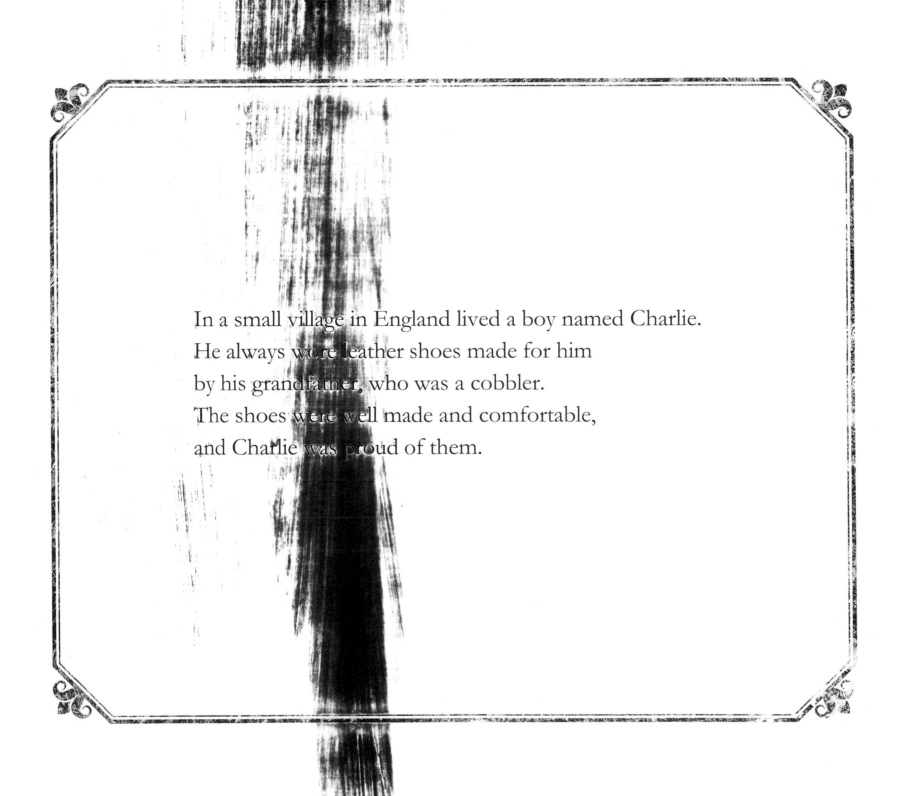

In a small village in England lived a boy named Charlie.
He always wore leather shoes made for him
by his grandfather, who was a cobbler.
The shoes were well made and comfortable,
and Charlie was proud of them.

But people were leaving
the small village. One family
after another moved away
until the village was almost empty.
There was no one to buy
Grandfather's shoes,
and by the end of winter,
Charlie's family decided
to move to the city of Manchester.

The train station was crowded with people, all going to the city to find jobs.

Charlie didn't want to leave home. His dad said to Grandfather, "Don't worry. There are many textile factories. I'm sure I'll find work there."

Then the train pulled into the station, hissing smoke and steam. It was time to go.

When they arrived in Manchester, Charlie and his brother Edward could not believe their eyes.

They saw a sea of moving people and tall buildings everywhere reaching up to the gray sky.

Charlie's family moved to an area called Angel Meadow,
but there was no green meadow to welcome them.
Their rooms were in an old, dark tenement building.
It was three stories high and housed several other families.
The sun never shone on that Angel Meadow house.

Nobody there wore leather shoes like Charlie's,
but Charlie didn't care that he was different.
Every step he took on those dark, muddy streets
reminded him of his village and his grandfather.
He would look down at his shoes and think,
"One day, I'm going to make shoes too."

Charlie's family worked
in a textile factory where huge
machines clanked all day,
turning out rolls of fabric.
Everyone had to work hard
to keep up with the machines,
and Charlie and the other
children had to clean
the machines and carry coal.

The factory workers called Charlie
"Leather Shoe Charlie" because wherever he went,
his leather shoes went *click, click, click.*

"Oy! Leather Shoe Charlie! Take this bolt of cloth!"

"Yes, sir!"

"Come over here, Leather Shoe Charlie!"

"Yes, sir!"

Life in Manchester
was different from the
village. Nights were spent
working late at the factory,
and the air was always gray
with thick chimney smoke.

Mom coughed and coughed,
and did not seem to get better.
Dad looked as though
he was getting smaller.

The bad conditions at the factory
made Mom's cough worse.
No one got the rest they needed,
but they didn't dare say anything.
If they complained to the boss,
they could lose their jobs.
There were plenty of people
waiting outside the factory
for a chance to work.

Charlie heard some women telling
Mom: "Tea is good for a cough."

"Who can afford to buy tea
with the money we make?" said Mom.

On Saturday evening, Charlie
and his mother went to the night
market near the factory.
The market sold all sorts of things,
such as flour, potatoes, salt, and oats.
While Mom bought groceries,
Charlie looked for some tea.
But it was very expensive,
and he didn't have enough money.

That night, Mom coughed for hours.
Charlie slipped out of bed
and went back to the market.
"Sir, I'd like to exchange these shoes
for some tea. They're good shoes,
made of sturdy leather by my grandfather."

The man said, "Do you really want
to exchange them for some tea?"

Charlie nodded.

The shop owner took the shoes
and handed Charlie a box of tea.

Charlie woke up early, got out of bed,
and boiled some water in the kettle.
He made a cup of hot tea
and gave it to his mother.

"Charlie, where did you get this?"
she asked him.

He looked at his feet.

Even without his shoes,
he still thought of himself
as Leather Shoe Charlie.

One day he would make shoes
just like his grandfather
and walk again, *click, click, click,*
in beautiful leather shoes.

The Industrial Revolution

The story of Leather Shoe Charlie takes place in England during early days of the Industrial Revolution, a time of rapid social and economic change. From roughly 1760 to 1840, a large number of high-powered machines were invented, allowing goods to be made faster, easier, and cheaper.

Before the Industrial Revolution, most English people lived in rural communities. Farming was the primary way of life. Handmade items, like Charlie's shoes, were bought and sold in small villages. Craftspeople made one item at time — a slow and labor-intensive process.

The Industrial Revolution brought new manufacturing technologies, which used energy from steam and coal. Machines completed tasks that would have taken fifty men to accomplish. As a result of this technological boom, thousands of families left their farms to earn wages working in coal mines or factories.

With millions of people entering the workforce, city landscapes changed, and businesses were able to expand. Scientists and engineers invented machines that could create products more cost-effectively and efficiently than ever before. The increased population of workers and new technological advancements gave business owners the opportunity to achieve maximum production.

The mass-produced goods manufactured by England's factories and mills needed to be transported to other parts of the world, and so a global system of industry and trade developed during the Industrial Revolution. Countries all over the world were soon linked together by railroads, steamships, canals, and tunnels, allowing goods to be sold on a global scale.

Working and Living Conditions

Due to the large population shift during the Industrial Revolution, the structure of English society was completely reorganized. With new innovations and plenty of workers, businessman became wealthy, thus developing a rich upper class. Their employees, however, were often neglected and poorly paid.

Workers who left their villages and farms looking for a new start found instead crowded urban tenements like Angel Meadow. Families of up to ten people lived in a single room with little to eat or drink. Sickness and disease spread rapidly in the polluted environment.

Textile mills posed their own difficulties. Not only did men and women have to endure fourteen-hour workdays in hot, noisy factories, but children did as well. Younger workers were recruited because they could squeeze into tight spaces to replace loose spools or clean out clogged machinery.

People working in coal mines also experienced unhealthy working conditions. Miners breathed in deadly toxins as they worked long hours in the darkness. Many young workers lost limbs and even died working in the mills and mines. Eventually, laws were passed to protect children from abusive labor practices.

Key Terms and Concepts

Industrialization is the process by which an economy is transformed from primarily agricultural to one based on the manufacturing of goods.

Mass production, the creation of goods in large amounts, reduces both the time and cost needed to create a product, and thus results in higher profits.

Tenements, apartment buildings that housed workers as cities industrialized, often featured crowded, difficult living conditions.

The Industrial Revolution created a new social class structure. There were severe **social inequities**, or disparities in wealth and power, between the affluent merchants and the masses of factory workers.

A **cottage industry** is a business or manufacturing activity carried on in a person's home. With the onset of the Industrial Revolution, this type of lifestyle and business practice largely became obsolete.

The Beginning of a Global Economy

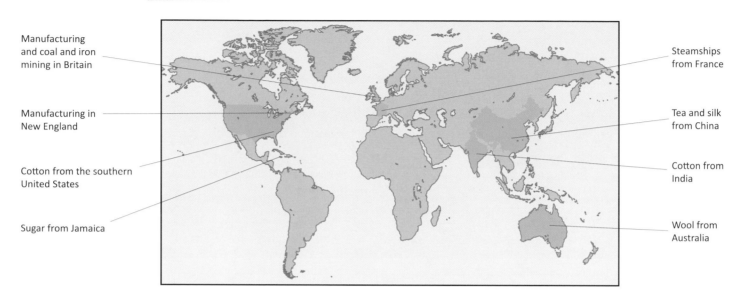

Manufacturing and coal and iron mining in Britain

Manufacturing in New England

Cotton from the southern United States

Sugar from Jamaica

Steamships from France

Tea and silk from China

Cotton from India

Wool from Australia

The map above shows how the Industrial Revolution linked countries all over the world together through manufacturing, technology, and enterprise. Countries could mass produce their goods and sell them to other parts of the world. This type of business trading and technological exchange between countries is known as **globalization**, *which is a common practice of enterprise today.*

A Changing Population

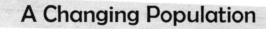

1801

- 85% Living in Rural Areas
- 15% Living in Urban Areas

1900

- 15% Living in Rural Areas
- 85% Living in Urban Areas

Before the Industrial Revolution, most of Britain's population lived in rural areas, but by the end of it, most people had chosen to move to cities. Britain's population also experienced substantial growth during this time. In 1801, when Britain's first census was taken, the total population was about 10 million. By 1900, the population had grown to nearly 40 million.

A Timeline of Events

1712   Thomas Newcomen (English) invents the first steam engine.

1759   The first Canal Act is passed, enabling the Duke of Bridgewater (English) to link his coal mining business in Worsley with Manchester.

1764   James Hargreaves (English) invents the spinning jenny, which enabled cloth to be made faster and more easily.

1771   Richard Arkwright (English) establishes the world's first factory — a large water-powered textile mill.

1790   Samuel Slater (English-American) opens America's first water-powered cotton spinning mill. Soon after, America experiences its own Industrial Revolution.

1793   Eli Whitney (American) invents the cotton gin, allowing cotton to be produced in a more efficient manner.

1802   Sir Robert Peel (English) introduces the Health and Morals of Apprentices Act, designed to improve working conditions for apprentices in the cotton mills. This act did not address the working conditions of "free children."

1804   Richard Trevithick (English) debuts the first steam-powered locomotive.

1807   Robert Fulton (American) builds the first successful steamship.

1819   The Cotton Mills and Factories Act is passed in England, establishing nine as the minimum working age, and the maximum working hours at twelve.

1847   The Ten Hours Act is passed in England, limiting the working hours of women and children to ten hours per day.

1856   Sir Henry Bessemer (English) develops a process to make steel in an inexpensive way.

1938   The Fair Labor Standards Act is passed in the United States, establishing minimum wage, overtime pay, and child labor standards.

MANCHESTER